AND THE **PIZZA**
OF **PERIL**

Look for Stinkbomb and Ketchup-Face's previous kerfuffles:

❧ • ❧

*Stinkbomb and Ketchup-Face and
the Badness of Badgers*

*Stinkbomb and Ketchup-Face and
the Quest for the Magic Porcupine*

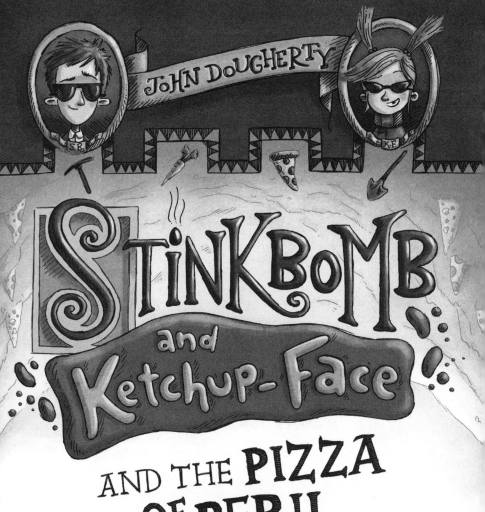

STINKBOMB
and
Ketchup-Face

AND THE PIZZA OF PERIL

JOHN DOUGHERTY

ILLUSTRATED BY SAM RICKS

putnam

G. P. PUTNAM'S SONS

G. P. PUTNAM'S SONS

an imprint of Penguin Random House LLC
375 Hudson Street
New York, NY 10014

Text copyright © 2015 by John Dougherty.
Illustrations copyright © 2019 by Sam Ricks.
First published as *Stinkbomb and Ketchup-Face and the Evilness of Pizza* in
Great Britain by Oxford University Press.
First American edition published in 2019 by G. P. Putnam's Sons.

Library of Congress Cataloging-in-Publication Data
Names: Dougherty, John, author. I Ricks, Sam, illustrator.
Title: Stinkbomb and Ketchup-Face and the pizza of peril / John Dougherty ; illustrated
by Sam Ricks. Description: First American edition. I New York, NY : G. P. Putnam's
Sons, 2019. Summary: "Siblings Stinkbomb and Ketchup-Face set out to save the
library by thwarting the rascally international badgers intent on mining the pizza
caves for cash"—Provided by publisher. Identifiers: LCCN 2017054155 (print) I LCCN
2018000321 (ebook) I ISBN 9780525515647 (ebook) I ISBN 9780525515630
(hardcover) Subjects: I CYAC: Brothers and sisters—Fiction. I Adventure and
adventurers—Fiction. I Libraries—Fiction. I Badgers—Fiction. I Humorous stories.
Classification: LCC PZ7.D74433 (ebook) I LCC PZ7.D74433 Stp 2019 (print) I DDC
[Fic]—dc23
LC record available at https://lccn.loc.gov/2017054155
Printed in the United States of America. ISBN 9780525515630
10 9 8 7 6 5 4 3 2 1

Design by Eileen Savage. Text set in Warnock Pro.

As always, to Noah & Cara,
with lots of love and buns.
And, as promised, to my wonderful
godson Myles and his equally lovely
siblings, Hannah & Matthew.
—J.D.

For Anna, who likes
pizza and absurdity.
—S.R.

TOP SECRET CASE FILES

The Great Kerfuffle Secret Service
Persons of Interest

TOP SECRET

@ BKRFFL

Stinkbomb

- Occupation: *Boy*
- Known associates: *Ketchup-Face (younger sister)*
- Interests: *Interesting things, thwarting badgers*
- Distinguishing characteristics: *Very large pockets containing lots of interesting things*

Ketchup-Face

- Occupation: *Girl*
- Known associates: *Stinkbomb (older brother)*
- Interests: *Singing, jam, ketchup, pretend horseys*
- Distinguishing characteristics: *Gap where she recently lost a tooth*

TOP SECRET

King Toothbrush Weasel

- **Occupation:** *King of Great Kerfuffle*
- **Known associates:** *The army of Great Kerfuffle (otherwise known as Malcolm the Cat)*
- **Interests:** *Reigning, being royal, kinging*
- **Distinguishing characteristics:** *Crown, ceremonial beard*

Malcolm the Cat

- **Occupation:** *Army*
  (no, really, he's the entire army)
- **Known associates:** *Likes to pretend he doesn't have any*
- **Interests:** *Eating, sleeping, tormenting small helpless creatures, tormenting big helpful creatures*
- **Distinguishing characteristics:** *Gray fur, red soldier's jacket, unblinking stare*

The Little Shopping Cart

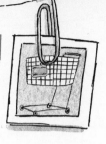

- Occupation: Shopping cart

- Known associates: Stinkbomb & Ketchup-Face, King Toothbrush Weasel

- Interests: Being helpful, veering to one side

- Distinguishing characteristics: None. One shopping cart looks just like another. Oh, apart from being little, I suppose. But definitely not a horsey.

Miss Butterworth

- Occupation: Librarian

- Known associates: The Ancient Order of Ninja Librarians; Miss Tibbles, who runs Bouncy Sing & Clap Story Time for Toddlers

- Interests: Wisdom, knowledge, stories

- Distinguishing characteristics: Hard to tell, since she dresses all in black from head to toe, apart from her eyes. Which are smiley and kind.

The Badgers

- Occupation: Badgers

- Known associates: Each other

- Interests: Being evil and wicked, doing bad things, villainy, worms and garbage cans, pretending not to be badgers

- Distinguishing characteristics: They look like badgers

"GET OUT OF JAIL FREE"

CHAPTER I

———— • ————

IN WHICH
OUR HEROES WAKE UP,
AND SOME STUFF HAPPENS

It was the quietest hour, when night covers the world like a blanket. Above the peaceful little island of Great Kerfuffle, stars **shimmered** like silver sequins against the velvet blackness. Below, the earth was silent. Not a creature stirred; all was still.

Then the sun popped **up** over the horizon like a jolly potato, and morning started.

And in a tall tree in the yard of a lovely house high on a hillside above the tiny village of Loose

1

Pebbles, a blackbird, was **singing** in the shower. Trees don't usually have showers, of course, but the blackbird wanted to be clean for the start of the story, so it had had one installed.

Inside the lovely house, in a beautiful pink bedroom, a little girl called Ketchup-Face was sleeping peacefully . . . until the blackbird turned the tap all the way up to "extra splooshy" and began **twittering** at the top of its voice. At that, Ketchup-Face stopped sleeping peacefully and jumped out of bed, extremely unpeacefully.

"**Hey!**
BLACKBIRD!

"Zip it!"

she yelled, running toward the window. **"Ow,"** she added, as the soap the blackbird had just thrown at her bounced off her forehead. **"Waaaaaauuugggghh!"** she continued as she stepped on the soap and, arms waving frantically, skidded across the room. **"Oof,"** she concluded, banging her nose against the window frame.

The blackbird, grinning hugely, stuck out its tongue and blew a **raspberry**. Then it rinsed off the suds, turned off the shower, dried itself with a little towel, and flew away.

Rubbing her nose, Ketchup-Face went to wake her brother.

Ketchup-Face's brother was named Stinkbomb, and seconds later he woke to find his sister trying to tie a knot in his legs.

"What," he demanded grumpily, "are you doing?"

"I'm trying to tie a knot in your legs," Ketchup-Face explained.

"Why?" Stinkbomb grouched.

"To see if I can," Ketchup-Face answered, frowning and poking her tongue out of the corner of her mouth.

Stinkbomb thought about this. The idea of having a knot tied in his legs certainly sounded interesting, but he wasn't sure if he would actually like it. So he decided to throw a pillow at his sister.

"Oof," said Ketchup-Face through a faceful of pillow, falling over backward. "What did you do that for?"

"I don't want you to tie a knot in my legs," Stinkbomb explained.

"Why not?"

"Because if there's a knot in my legs, I won't be able to put my pants on. And if we have an adventure when there's a knot in my legs, I won't be able to run away from the bad guys."

"Okay," said Ketchup-Face, getting up. "Do you think we're going to have an adventure?"

"I should think so," said Stinkbomb wisely. "It feels like that sort of story."

And just then, there was a **knock** on the door.

CHAPTER 2

—·—

IN WHICH
THE DOOR IS ANSWERED,
AND THE ADVENTURE BEGINS

Only thirteen words later, Stinkbomb and Ketchup-Face had shoved themselves into their clothes. Racing to the front door, they flung it open. There, on the threshold, was a little shopping cart wearing a pair of dark glasses.

"Starlight!" Ketchup-Face said delightedly. "My horsey!"

"*Shhh!*" **hissed** the little shopping cart. "I don't want anyone to know it's me! I'm in disguise!"

Stinkbomb looked around carefully, and

then leaned closer. "But your name isn't really Starlight," he pointed out quietly. "And you're not really a horsey."

"You could pretend to be," added Ketchup-Face in a cheerful whisper. "If you don't want people to know it's you."

"Fair point," the little shopping cart admitted after a moment's thought. Then, more loudly, it added, "Er, yes, that's right. It's me, Starlight. The, er, horsey. **Whinny, whinny, neigh, neigh.** Um . . . got any carrots?"

"I might," Stinkbomb said, feeling around in his pockets. Stinkbomb was the sort of boy who kept all kinds of useful things in his pockets, and quite a lot of useless things as well. "Yes, here you are." He produced a large carrot and jammed it between two of the wires of the basket, a little below the sunglasses.

"Thanks," said the little shopping cart. "Er . . . yum. I love carrots. **Neigh, whinny, whinny, neigh.** I'm a horse. All right, hop in."

Stinkbomb and Ketchup-Face scrambled into

the basket, and seconds later they were galloping across the fields like two children in a little shopping cart.

"Why the disguise?" Stinkbomb wanted to know.

"Well," the little shopping cart said modestly, "I'm doing a job for the Great Kerfuffle **Secret Service.**"

"**Wow!**" said Stinkbomb, impressed. Then, feeling that this didn't convey just *how* impressed he was, he said, "**Wowsers!**" This still didn't seem quite enough, so after a moment's thought he added, **"Wowsers my trousers!"**

This felt more like it. "So, where are we going?"

"We're going to the headquarters of the Great Kerfuffle **Secret Service**," the little shopping cart whispered, and just at that moment they drew up outside King Toothbrush Weasel's palace. Pinned to the gate was a piece of paper on which someone had written:

Headquarters
of the
Great Kerfuffle
Secret Service

King Toothbrush Weasel was the king of the little island of Great Kerfuffle, and his palace was about the size of a small cottage. It had pretty little towers with thatched turrets, and dinky little battlements, and the sweetest little sentry box you've ever seen. The sentry box was usually full of the entire army of Great Kerfuffle, who was a small cat named Malcolm the Cat, but at the moment it was empty. As the little shopping cart **screeched** to a halt in what it hoped was a daring and **secret-agentish** sort of way, Stinkbomb and Ketchup-Face leapt from its basket and ran to the door.

"Wait!" the little shopping cart said. "They won't let you in unless you do the **secret knock!**"

"Wowsers my trousers!" said Stinkbomb, feeling that this adventure was getting more exciting by the minute, and hoping that before long it would involve **disguises** and **gadgets** and **foreign spies**. "What's the **secret knock?**"

The little shopping cart shrugged. "I don't know," it said. "It's a **secret**."

Ketchup-Face waved her fist very near to the door without touching it. "That's a **secret knock**," she said. "It's so **secret** you can't even hear it."

"But if nobody can hear it," said Stinkbomb, "how will the person on the other side of the door know you've **knocked**?"

Ketchup-Face scratched her head. "Um . . . don't know," she said cheerily. "Why don't you try?"

"Okay," agreed Stinkbomb. Thinking hard, he raised his hand to the knocker and **knocked** the most **secret** and complicated **knock** he could think of. It went:

Knock . . .
Knock-knock knockity knock . . .
Knock kno-knock knock-knock-knock . . .
Knock-knock, **knock-knock,** knock knock
knockity knock knock knock . . .
Knock knock kno-knock knock,
knock kno-knock kno-knock . . .

Knock knock knock knock . . . knock . . .
Knock knock knock,
knockkkkkk knockkkkkk knockkkk,
knock knock knock . . .

. . .

Knock knock . . .

. . .

. . . knock . . .

Knock!!!!!!
Knock!!!!!!
Knock!!!!!!!

. . . knock knock knock knock knock knock
knock knock knock knock . . .

Tap tap tippity tippity tap tap tap . . .

Knock knock

Tap

Knock knock

Tap

Knock knock

Tap tap tippity tippity tap tap tap

**Knock knock kno-knock knock knock,
knocky knock knock, knock knock . . .**

. . .
. . .
. . .
. . .
. . .
. . .
. . .
. . .
. . .
. . .

. . .

. . .

. . .

. . .

. . .

. . .

. . .

. . .

. . .

. . .

. . .

. . .

Knock.

He stood back, like an artist admiring his work, and then, after a moment's thought, stepped back up to the door, lifted the knocker again, and added:

Knock kno-kno-knock knock, knock knock!

Then he stood back again, folded his arms, and waited.

CHAPTER 3

— · —

IN WHICH
THE DOOR IS ANSWERED

V ery soon there came a voice from behind
the door.

"Was that the **secret knock**?" it said.

"Yes," said Stinkbomb.

"Oh," said the voice. "I didn't think the **secret knock** was as long as that."

"Well, it is," Stinkbomb said. "I did it brilliantly, didn't I?"

"Yes," said the voice. "I don't know how you managed to remember it all."

"Actually," said Stinkbomb, "I might have gone a bit wrong in the middle. Shall I do it again?"

"Er, no, that's all right," the voice said quickly.

The door opened and there, wearing a pair of dark glasses, a serious expression, and a little badge, stood King Toothbrush Weasel.

"Hello, King Toothbrush Weasel," said Ketchup-Face brightly.

King Toothbrush Weasel gave her a stern look. "I am not King Toothbrush Weasel," he said firmly. He pointed at his badge, which said Head of Palace Security, and said, "I am the Head of Palace Security." Then he looked at the little shopping cart. "Why have you got a carrot jammed into the front of your basket?"

"It's a disguise," the shopping cart said.

King Toothbrush Weasel's forehead wrinkled in puzzlement. "Why have you disguised yourself as a carrot?"

"Er, no," the little shopping cart said shyly, "I'm disguised as a horse. **Neigh, whinny, neigh**."

"A *horse*?" said King Toothbrush Weasel. "Horses don't have carrots jammed in the front of their baskets."

"I'm pretending to eat it," explained the shopping cart.

King Toothbrush Weasel shook his head impatiently. "Horses don't eat carrots," he said. "They eat goldfish."

"No they don't!" protested Ketchup-Face.

"Yes they do," insisted King Toothbrush Weasel. "The horse climbs **up** a tree and sits on a branch, waiting for a nice fat goldfish to come **trotting** along, and when it does, the horse drops **down** out of the tree onto the goldfish and eats it up."

"I think you're thinking of jaguars," said

Stinkbomb politely. "But they drop onto deer, not goldfish."

"No," said King Toothbrush Weasel. "Jaguars don't *eat* deer; they turn *into* them. The deer lays eggs in a sort of jelly, which is called deerspawn, and they hatch out into jaguars, which swim around the pond until they grow legs and their tails drop off and they turn into deer."

"No, you silly king," Ketchup-Face said. "That's not jaguars and deers, it's frogs and **Ow!** what did

you do that for? I only said it was **OW!"**
she added as Stinkbomb elbowed her in the ribs
again.

"Let's not stand here arguing about animals,"
Stinkbomb hissed. "I want to get on with the
adventure."

"Okay," Ketchup-Face said. "I only said it was

 okay, okay, let's get on
with the adventure."

"Very well," agreed King Toothbrush Weasel.
"You'd better come in."

CHAPTER 4

— • —

IN WHICH
THEY GO IN

The hallway of King Toothbrush Weasel's palace was small and cluttered. King Toothbrush Weasel **squeezed** past a **bicycle** that was leaning against a **radiator**, and walked into a **broom closet**.

"Come along!" he said impatiently. Stinkbomb and Ketchup-Face looked at each other, shrugged, and followed, the little shopping cart **squeezing** in behind them.

"Why are we in a closet?" Ketchup-Face asked.

King Toothbrush Weasel gave her another stern look. "It is not a closet," he said firmly. "It is a **secret elevator**, which will **secretly** take us to the **secret headquarters** of the Great Kerfuffle **Secret Service**." He pressed a button

on the wall—quite a big button, which looked as if it had fallen off a cardigan or a woolly coat, and which was fastened to the wall with sticky tape—closed the door, and made a noise like an elevator.

After about thirty seconds, he stopped making a noise like an elevator, went, **"Ding!"**

and opened the door, and they all emerged into the hallway again.

"This way," King Toothbrush Weasel said, and led them all down the hallway, into the kitchen, around the table, back out into the hall again, and into the room opposite the broom closet. They waited politely while he took off his dark glasses and the little badge that said Head of Palace Security , put on a small crown and a badge that said King , and sat down on a comfy armchair that was trimmed with tinsel and had a label on it saying Throne .

"Good morning, Stinkbomb and Ketchup-Face," he said gravely. "I have called you here to meet with the Great Kerfuffle **Secret Service**."

"**Wowsers**," said Stinkbomb excitedly.

"**Wowsers my trousers!**"

"Gosh!" said Ketchup-Face. "Er . . .

GOSH MY PANTS!"

"As you know," King Toothbrush Weasel said, "all the badgers in Great Kerfuffle are in prison, having been found guilty of extreme naughtiness. But we think they are planning to escape."

"Oh," said Stinkbomb disappointedly, **"not the badgers again.** We've done them twice now. I thought this was a story about spies and things."

"Still," Ketchup-Face said, "at least we'll get to meet the **Secret Service**."

"That's true," said Stinkbomb, brightening.

"And here he is now!" said King Toothbrush Weasel.

The **Secret Service** came in. It was Malcolm the Cat in a pair of dark glasses.

"Oh," said Stinkbomb, disappointed again.

"Stinkbomb and Ketchup-Face," King Toothbrush Weasel said, "our special agent, **Double-O Malcolm the Cat**, has been on the **secret mission** of hanging around outside the jail all morning listening to the badgers." He turned to Malcolm the Cat. "Have you brought your report with you?"

Malcolm the Cat sat down on the rug and stared at the king without blinking. "Yes," he said eventually.

There was a long pause.

"Well..." said King Toothbrush Weasel, "could I see it, please?"

Malcolm the Cat stared at him some more. "All right," he said, standing up and producing a bright yellow folder with pictures of dead mice on it. He held the folder up so that they could all see it, and then put it on the rug and sat on it.

King Toothbrush Weasel sighed. "No, I mean, could I *read* it, please."

"Oh," said Malcolm the Cat. "Why didn't you say so?"

After the next pause had gone on for a bit,

King Toothbrush Weasel said, "So . . . *could* I read it, please?" After a further pause, he added impatiently, "Malcolm the Cat, give me your report!"

"All right, all right," said Malcolm the Cat. "Keep your pants on. Some people are so impatient." He slowly got up, stared down at the folder, licked his paw, washed carefully behind his ears, straightened his tail, brushed a bit of fluff off his sleeve, polished his buttons, picked up the folder, went into the kitchen, made himself a snack, ate the snack, did

the dishes, went to the shop, bought a newspaper, came back, licked his paw, washed carefully behind his ears, read the newspaper, did the crossword, wrote a letter to the editor, did the sudoku, licked his paw, and washed carefully behind his ears. Then he held the folder out. "Here you are," he said. "Oh, wait," he added, taking it back. "Is this the right folder?" He opened it up and looked inside, carefully checking the contents three times. Apparently satisfied, he closed the folder and held it out again. "Here you are," he said again. "Or maybe you aren't," he added, snatching it away as King

Toothbrush Weasel reached for it. "No, my mistake, here it is." He held the newspaper out and gave it to King Toothbrush Weasel.

"At last," said King Toothbrush Weasel. "Thank you." He opened it up and began to read it. "Wait a minute," he said. "This isn't your report. It's the newspaper."

"Oh, sorry," said Malcolm the Cat innocently. "I don't know how that happened. Now, where did I put that report?"

"It's in your paw," said Stinkbomb.

"No it isn't," said Malcolm the Cat, looking at his paw.

"No, the *other* paw," Stinkbomb said.

Malcolm the Cat looked at his back paw.

"No, the *front* paw," said Stinkbomb crossly. "No, the *other* front paw," he went on. **"Look!** *That* **paw!"**

"Oh, so it is," said Malcolm the Cat. "Here you are." He held the report out toward King Toothbrush Weasel, and then snatched it away again.

There was no telling how long this could have gone on if Stinkbomb hadn't suddenly remembered that he had a can of cat food in his pocket. He reached into his pocket, pulled out the can of cat food, and dropped it on Malcolm the Cat's tail.

"**Ow!**" yelped Malcolm the Cat, and let go of the folder. Quickly, Stinkbomb snatched it up and gave it to the king.

CHAPTER 5

— • —

IN WHICH
WE FINALLY FIND OUT
WHAT WAS IN MALCOLM THE CAT'S REPORT

King Toothbrush Weasel opened Malcolm the Cat's folder and pulled out a thick wad of paper. On the front was written in large letters:

TOP SECRET FILES

Malcolm the Cat's
Secret Mission Report

"Right," said King Toothbrush Weasel. "Listen carefully, Stinkbomb and Ketchup-Face." He flipped to the next page and began to read aloud:

MY REPORT
by Malcolm the Cat

The following is everything I heard the badgers say while I was on my secret mission of hanging around outside the jail listening to them.

"Whisper,
      whisper,
                  mutter,
            mutter,

SHUT UP, EVERYONE,
THERE'S MALCOLM THE CAT!"

King Toothbrush Weasel paused, and flipped the page over. Then he flipped to the next page, and the next, and the next. When he had flipped over the very last page, he looked up impatiently. "Malcolm the Cat," he said, "all the rest of the pages are blank."

Malcolm the Cat shrugged. "They didn't say anything else," he said.

Stinkbomb sighed. "Come on," he said. "This must be the part where we go to the jail to see for ourselves what they're up to."

CHAPTER 6

—·—

IN WHICH
WE SEE WHAT THE BADGERS ARE UP TO

Meanwhile, in the jail in the little village of Loose Pebbles, the badgers were plotting.

"If only we had a shovel," said Rolf the Badger, a big badger with a big badge that said BIG BADGER . "Then we could dig our way out."

"Good idea, Rolf the Badger," said Harry the Badger, taking a sip of tea from a mug marked World's Best Badger . "How could we get a shovel?"

"Well," suggested Stewart the Badger, the

smallest of the badgers, "we could go to the store and buy one."

Harry the Badger sighed. "We can't go to the store and buy a shovel," he said.

"Oh," said Stewart the Badger. "Why not?"

"Because we're in prison," explained Harry the Badger.

"Oh," said Stewart the Badger. "Maybe we could dig our way out, and then go to the store and buy a shovel?"

"And how," asked Harry the Badger impatiently, "are we going to dig our way out?"

Stewart the Badger **scratched** his head. "Um . . . With a shovel?"

Harry the Badger sighed again. "Has anyone else got any **stupid** ideas?" he said sarcastically.

"Oooh! Me! Me!, I've got a stupid idea!"

said all the other badgers at once, and they began to tell Harry the Badger their **stupid** ideas. Some of them really were very **stupid** ideas indeed.

Harry the Badger held up his paws for silence. "Maybe I wasn't very clear," he said, cutting off a particularly **stupid** idea about a cup of coffee and a flying jellyfish. "When I said, 'Has anyone else got any **stupid** ideas?' what I really meant was 'Shut up.'"

"Oh, okay," said the other badgers, and they all shut up.

"Now," said Harry the Badger, "if we can't dig our way out, we're going to have to find some other way of escaping. Let's see." He looked at the floor. "We can't go down without a shovel . . ." He looked at the door. "We can't go forward without a key . . ." He turned around and looked at the wall. "We can't go backward without, um, a thing for smashing holes in walls . . ." He looked **up** at the ceiling. It was quite a long way up, and right in the middle of it was a small square skylight. "Ah-*hah*!" he said meaningfully.

"Er, no," said Stewart the Badger helpfully. "That's not a *hah*. It's a window."

Harry the Badger sighed. "Maybe I wasn't

very clear," he said. "When I said, 'Ah-*hah*!' what I really meant was 'Oh, look, there's a skylight. Maybe we could make a tower of badgers and climb out of it.'"

"Oh, okay," said the other badgers, and they made a tower of badgers. It was a very tall, thin tower of badgers, but it didn't quite reach the skylight.

"Bother," said Harry the Badger. "If only we had something to stand on."

"What about the game cabinet?" said Rolf the Badger from somewhere underneath Harry the Badger. He pointed at the small cabinet full of games that sat in the corner of the jail. "We could move that and stand on it."

"Oh, no," said Stewart the Badger from somewhere underneath Rolf the Badger. "We mustn't move the game cabinet."

"Why not?" said Harry the Badger.

"Because someone might fall down the hole," explained Stewart the Badger.

The other badgers stared so hard at Stewart

the Badger that they all lost their balance and the tower collapsed, spilling badgers all over the floor. Harry the Badger picked himself up again. "What hole?" he demanded.

"Well," said Stewart the Badger, "when we first got put in prison, I noticed there was a big hole in the floor. So I moved the game cabinet on top of it so that no one would fall down it."

Harry the Badger took a deep breath and let it out very slowly. "This . . . hole," he said, in an odd sort of voice. "Would it be big enough for, say, a badger to get through?"

Stewart the Badger nodded. "Oh, yes," he said cheerfully.

Harry the Badger took another big breath and let it out even more slowly. Then, in the same odd voice, he said, "And . . . do you think the hole goes a long way down?"

Stewart the Badger nodded again. "It looked like it went *ever* such a long way," he said.

Harry the Badger took a third big breath and let it out more slowly still. "All the way out of the prison, perhaps?"

"Oh, yes," said Stewart the Badger.

Harry the Badger took a fourth big breath and forgot to let it out at all. After a while he went purple and made a funny squeaky noise, and then he remembered and let it all out at once. "Did it not occur to you that a big hole that goes all the way out of prison might be useful to badgers who are locked up *in* prison?"

"Nope," said Stewart the Badger. Then his eyes widened. "Wait a minute!" he said. "If the hole's big enough for a badger to get through . . ."

"*Ye*-es?" said Harry the Badger.

" . . . and if it goes all the way out of prison . . ."

"*Ye*-es?" said Harry the Badger.

" . . . then a badger could go through the hole . . ."

"*Ye*-es?" said Harry the Badger.

" . . . and get all the way out of prison . . ."

"*Ye*-es?" said Harry the Badger.

" . . . and go to the store and buy a shovel!" said Stewart the Badger. "And then we could dig a hole and escape from prison!"

"Well, yes," said Harry the Badger.

There was a long pause, during which nobody

"Or we could just USE THE HOLE THAT'S BEEN HERE ALL THE TIME, AND GET OUT OF PRISON THAT WAY!!!!!!"

spoke or moved or went to the bathroom, and then Stewart the Badger said, "Oh, *yeah*!"

And then all the other badgers said, "Oh, *yeah*!" as well, because they'd only just understood it, too; and they rushed over to the corner and dragged the game cabinet out of the way, and revealed the hole.

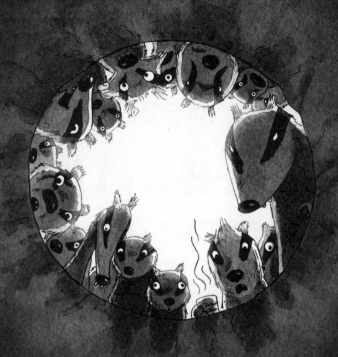

CHAPTER 7

IN WHICH
THE BADGERS ESCAPE
FROM PRISON

The badgers all gathered around the hole and looked down.

"How far do you think it goes?" asked Rolf the Badger.

"All the way to the bottom, I reckon," said Harry the Badger.

"The bottom of what?" asked Stewart the Badger.

"The bottom of the hole, of course," said Harry the Badger. "Right, Stewart the Badger: off you go. Tell us when you get to the bottom."

"Okay," said Stewart the Badger, clambering into the hole. "It's very deep," he went on, fumbling in the gloom for a paw-hold.

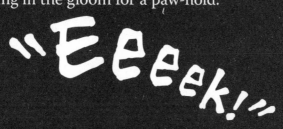

he added, plummeting into the darkness. **"Oof!"** he concluded, landing on his back at the bottom of the hole. "Er . . . I'm at the bottom!"

There was a skidding noise in the darkness above him, and moments later he said **"Oof!"** again as something large and warm and badgery dropped out of the shaft and landed on his tummy.

The badger on Stewart the Badger's tummy

peered down at Stewart the Badger, and suddenly realized that this was his big chance. For two whole books, all he had done was the same things as the other badgers. He hadn't even been given a name. Now here he was, all alone with one of the stars of the stories! Maybe they would have a proper conversation, and he would say something really important, and Stewart the Badger would say his name, and then all the readers would know who he was, and love him, and demand he be brought back in the next book, and he would be a star!

Unfortunately, he got so excited at the thought of being a proper character that he just sat there on Stewart the Badger's tummy, quivering with excitement, and then shouted out the first thing that came into his head, which—for reasons he could never properly explain afterward—was

"Sam Churchill!"

Stewart the Badger stared **up** at him in bemusement, but before he could even ask *Who's Sam Churchill?* the badger on his tummy added, *Oof!* as another badger plummeted out of the darkness and landed on him, and his chance of glory was gone forever. And then the newly arrived badger said, *Oof!* as some more badgers arrived, and then those badgers said, *Oof!* and for several minutes nothing could be heard but the sound of badgers saying *Oof!* as other badgers fell on them.

By the time Stinkbomb and Ketchup-Face reached the jail, it was empty, and there were no badgers to be seen.

CHAPTER 8

—·—

IN WHICH
THE BADGERS MAKE A DISCOVERY

When all the badgers had finally finished falling onto other badgers and having other badgers fall onto them, they lay in a crumpled heap for a while, recovering. Eventually, Stewart the Badger got up. Since he was at the bottom of the pile of badgers, it fell over with a lot of **"Oof!"**s, and most of the badgers had to lie down and recover again.

But after some time, the badgers all got to their paws. As their eyes adjusted to the darkness, they realized that they were in a long underground tunnel.

"Hey," said Rolf the Badger. "These tunnel walls are all stripy!"

"Oh, yeah!" said all the other badgers.

And then Stewart the Badger said, "And they're quite tasty, too!"

Harry the Badger clipped him on the ear. "How many times have I told you not to eat the walls, Stewart the Badger?"

Stewart the Badger thought about this, and then he began to count very slowly on his paws, and then he said, "Er . . . None!"

"True," said Harry the Badger, "but that's not the point. Eating walls is very bad for you."

"Okay," agreed Stewart the Badger, eating the walls.

Harry the Badger clipped him on the ear again. "I said, don't!" he explained.

"What if the walls are made of food?" said Stewart the Badger.

Harry the Badger sighed. "Well, obviously you can eat the walls if they're made of food!" he said.

"Okay," agreed Stewart the Badger, eating the walls.

"But walls are never made of food!" Harry the Badger said.

"These are," said Stewart the Badger, eating the walls.

"Oh, so they are!" said all the other badgers, eating the walls.

And then Rolf the Badger said, "Wait a minute! I know where we are! We're in the legendary abandoned pizza mines of Great Kerfuffle!"

Harry the Badger stared at him. "What makes you think that, Rolf the Badger?"

"Because there's a sign over there that says

Legendary Abandoned
Pizza Mines of Great Kerfuffle

"See," said Rolf the Badger, pointing at it.

"So there is," said Harry the Badger, eating the walls. "Mmmm! Pizza!"

CHAPTER 9

— · —

IN WHICH
THE BADGERS STOP EATING THE WALLS, AND HARRY THE BADGER HAS AN IDEA

Some time later, a large number of very full badgers lay on the ground in the underground tunnel, burping and rubbing their tummies.

"Well," said Rolf the Badger, "that's the tastiest wall I ever tasted."

"Nearly as good as worms and that stuff you find in garbage cans!" said Stewart the Badger.

"I found some pizza in a garbage can once," said Rolf the Badger. He licked his paws and sighed. "I reckon these walls taste just as good."

"We could stay here forever!" Stewart the Badger said. "There's enough pizza in these mines to keep us going for the rest of our lives!"

"Yeah," said Harry the Badger, cunningly. "Or . . .

we could make a fortune!"

All the other badgers sat up.

"Just think about it," Harry the Badger continued. "All these pizzas, waiting to be dug up. And if we dig them up, we can sell them and make a fortune! And you know what we could do with a fortune?"

There was a pause while all the other badgers thought about it, and then Stewart the Badger said, "Um . . . We could buy lots of pizzas?"

"Yeah, we could," agreed Harry the Badger. "But that'd be stupid."

"Well, what, then?" asked Rolf the Badger.

Harry the Badger tutted impatiently. "What do us badgers love to do?" he asked.

"Um . . ." said all the other badgers.

Harry the Badger tutted again and handed Rolf the Badger a copy of STINKBOMB AND KETCHUP-FACE AND THE BADNESS OF BADGERS. Rolf the Badger flicked through the first few pages, reading slowly to himself. "Er . . . It says here that we

53

dig holes in the lawn and eat all the worms, and we knock over garbage cans and frighten chickens and drive too fast."

"Oh, yeah!" said all the other badgers.

"Exactly!" said Harry the Badger. "If we had a fortune, we could buy all the lawns we wanted and dig them up, and we could buy all the worms we wanted and eat them, and we could buy all the garbage cans we wanted and knock them over, and we could buy all the chickens we wanted and frighten them, and we could buy all the cars we wanted and drive them too fast!"

"And we could buy all the money we wanted and spend it on lawns and worms and garbage cans and chickens and cars!" said Stewart the Badger excitedly.

"Er . . . yeah," said Harry the Badger. "So what do you say, badgers? Who wants to make a fortune?"

"Me! Me!"

said all the other badgers excitedly. And they rushed off to see if the legendary abandoned pizza mines of Great Kerfuffle held any legendary abandoned pizza-mining equipment.

CHAPTER 10

———•———

IN WHICH
NOTHING MUCH HAPPENS

Meanwhile, Stinkbomb and Ketchup-Face were a little fed up, because even though it was their story, absolutely nothing seemed to be happening in it.

In fact, nothing at all happened for a few days, so those of you who are easily bored might want to skip to the next chapter right now.

However, for those of you who want to get an idea of how fed up they were, we're going to have an intermission.

Welcome to the intermission. Please stare at this lovely picture until next Tuesday.

Thank you. Now on with the story.

CHAPTER 11

—— • ——

IN WHICH
THERE IS PIZZA FOR LUNCH

A few days later, King Toothbrush Weasel summoned Stinkbomb and Ketchup-Face to the palace.

"It's very strange," said King Toothbrush Weasel. "The **Secret Service** has searched the whole island for the badgers, but it's as if they've vanished."

Just then, there was a knock at the door.

"Oh," said King Toothbrush Weasel, "that'll be the pizzas I ordered. Could somebody go to the door? Here's the money."

Stinkbomb took the money and went to the door. There, on the threshold, stood the pizza delivery man. He was a big pizza delivery man with a big badge that said Big Pizza Delivery Man .

"Pizzas!" he said cheerfully. "One of everything on the menu, as requested."

"Thanks," said Stinkbomb. "How much is that?"

The pizza delivery man counted slowly on his paws. "Um . . . that'll be lots of money, please."

"Okay," said Stinkbomb, and he gave him lots of money.

"Thanks," said the pizza delivery man, and he went away.

"Yum!" said Ketchup-Face as Stinkbomb carried the tower of pizza boxes back into the throne room. "I love pizza!"

"Me too," said King Toothbrush Weasel. "I thought we could have some pizza while we try to work out what the badgers might be up to."

"I wonder what the badgers *are* up to," mused Ketchup-Face, opening a box. It was a nicely designed pizza box, with the words *Badger Pizzas* printed around a picture of a badger sipping from a mug marked .

"Yes," said Stinkbomb. "I can't help feeling we're missing something." He opened a big box with a picture of a big badger wearing a big badge that said . "Mmmm—what's this one?"

"That looks like the *pescatore*," said King Toothbrush Weasel, checking the delivery menu. "'Tuna, shrimp, and anchovies, with tomato sauce, mozzarella, and basil.'"

"*Pescatore!* My favorite!" said Malcolm the Cat happily, chasing a slice around the room and then pouncing on it. "Or am I thinking of *napoletana*?" he asked himself, letting it go. "No, wait, it's definitely *pescatore*," he decided, pouncing on it again. "Although maybe . . ."

"Ooh," Ketchup-Face said, "this one smells lovely!"

"I think that's *margherita*," said King Toothbrush Weasel, checking the menu again. "'Just tomatoes and mozzarella—but you've never tasted better,' it says here."

"Ooh—what about this one!" said Stinkbomb, getting carried away and opening all the boxes. "And this one! And this one!"

"Um . . ." said King Toothbrush Weasel, examining each box in turn. "That looks like a *quattro formaggio*: 'tomato sauce topped with four mouthwatering cheeses—mozzarella, pecorino, gorgonzola, and Great Kerfuffle's own specialty cheese, daftypants.' And that one . . . let me see . . . that's a *napoletana*: 'mozzarella, tomatoes, and lots of anchovies.'"

"Ewww," said Ketchup-Face, looking at the next pizza. "This one doesn't look very good."

"You're just being fussy," said Stinkbomb. "I might have a slice of that, just to show you."

"That one must be a *vermi e rifiuti*," said King Toothbrush Weasel. "'Tomatoes and mozzarella with a generous helping of worms, plus the finest bits of trash, smothered in our special garbage can sauce made by the **secret method** of filling a garbage can with **soggy** leftovers and then knocking it over. Perfect after a hard day at work frightening chickens and driving too fast.'"

Ketchup-Face looked smugly at Stinkbomb.

"Go on, then," she said. "Have a slice. Just to show me."

Stinkbomb thought about this. The idea of having a slice of pizza with a generous helping of worms, plus the finest bits of trash, smothered in special garbage can sauce made by the **secret method** of filling a garbage can with **soggy** leftovers and then knocking it over, certainly sounded interesting, but he wasn't sure if he would actually like it.

"Anyway," he said, "we're supposed to be

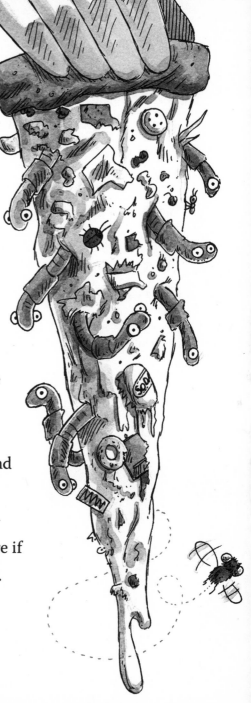

trying to work out where the badgers might be."

"But how are we supposed to do that?" said Ketchup-Face grumpily. "It's not as if we've got any clues or anything!"

Stinkbomb, Ketchup-Face, and King Toothbrush Weasel all sighed. For a moment there was silence, except for the sound of pizza being chewed.

And then they all heard a dreadful noise.

CHAPTER 12

—•—

IN WHICH
TERRIBLE DANGER THREATENS
THE LOOSE PEBBLES LIBRARY

Everyone ran to the window. The sound came again—a creaking, tearing sound, like a building in agony. They stared into the bright afternoon, trying to find the source of the sound.

And then Stinkbomb said, "Should the library be leaning over like that?"

There was another groaning, creaking sound, and the library tipped a little farther.

"Oh, no!" gasped Ketchup-Face.

"Follow me!" said King Toothbrush Weasel. "There's no time to lose!" And he led them out into the hallway, into the kitchen, around the table, back out into the hall, and into the closet, where he pressed the button on the wall. He closed the door and made a noise like an elevator, and then after about thirty seconds, he stopped making a noise like an elevator, went, **"Ding!"** and opened the door, and they all emerged into the hallway again. "Quickly!" he said urgently, leading them out into the sunlight just in time to see the little shopping cart screeching to a halt in front of the gate.

"To the Library!" yelled Ketchup-Face as they all scrambled into the basket.

"Hang on!" said Malcolm the Cat, and he ran back into the palace and returned with a stack of pizza boxes. "What?" he said as everyone tutted. "I'm hungry!"

"Do get in, Malcolm the Cat!" snapped King Toothbrush Weasel.

It took less than a sentence to reach the library, but already the great building was leaning over still farther.

"Look!" said Stinkbomb, pointing.

On the library roof, someone was tying a thick rope around the neck of a stone gargoyle.

"It's Miss Butterworth!" Ketchup-Face yelled excitedly. "She's a ninja librarian, and she's terribly brave and wise!"

"What are you telling me that for?" Stinkbomb asked. "I know who Miss Butterworth is!"

"Yes," agreed Ketchup-Face, "but some of the people reading the book might *not* know, so I'm telling *them*."

As the building creaked and groaned and tilted farther yet, Miss Butterworth—still holding the rope—raced down the now-diagonal wall and flung herself at the ground.

"Miss Butterworth!" Ketchup-Face screamed, but Miss Butterworth had calculated perfectly. The rope pulled taut just as her toes touched the

earth. Quickly, she fastened it around the leg of a passing elephant.

"Do you mind?" asked the elephant.

"*My apologies,*" puffed Miss Butterworth as Stinkbomb and Ketchup-Face rushed to meet her. "*But it is an emergency. It is only until the end of the story.*"

The elephant looked slightly put out. "I'm supposed to be in **Chapter Twenty-Eight**," it said. "Do you think you can untie me before then?"

"I hope so," Miss Butterworth said seriously. *"But danger threatens Great Kerfuffle, and at all costs the library must lean no farther."*

The elephant rolled its eyes grumpily.

King Toothbrush Weasel's face was solemn as he regarded the library. "We can't leave it like that forever," he said. "But the library is safe for now, thanks to that loyal and good-hearted armadillo."

"Elephant," said Stinkbomb.

"Where?" shrieked King Toothbrush Weasel, spinning on the spot and lifting the hem of his robe, as if worried that something small and poisonous might scurry up it and bite him. Then he glared at Stinkbomb. "This is no time for jokes," he said. "The whole of Great Kerfuffle is in terrible danger!"

"It is indeed," Miss Butterworth agreed. *"If the library tips over, the whole of Great Kerfuffle will capsize and we shall all be drowned in the sea."*

"Gosh," said Stinkbomb. "That's a bit serious for one of our stories, isn't it?"

"*Nevertheless,*" Miss Butterworth said, "*that is what will happen unless somebody goes beneath the library to find out what is happening.*"

CHAPTER 13

———•———

IN WHICH
SOMEBODY GOES BENEATH THE LIBRARY TO FIND OUT WHAT IS HAPPENING

Well," said King Toothbrush Weasel, "that sounds like a job for the **Secret Service**."

Everyone looked at the **Secret Service**, who was balanced on a large wobbly pile of pizza boxes.

"But I'm having my lunch!" protested the **Secret Service**, taking an entire pizza out of the top box and flinging it like a Frisbee in the direction of the library. "Hey! It's getting away!" With a tremendous leap, he sprang off the pile of boxes and brought the airborne pizza down just next to the elephant. "Got you!" he said triumphantly, and took a great bite. **"Ewww! Yuk!"** he added, spitting and gagging. **"Acckkk! Eccchhh!** *Vermi e rifiuti!"*

"Malcolm the Cat," said King Toothbrush Weasel sternly, "stop messing around. All your spitting and choking might distract this loyal and good-hearted armadillo . . ."

"Elephant," said the elephant.

"Where?" shrieked King Toothbrush Weasel, spinning on the spot and lifting the hem of his robe again. Then he glared at the elephant. "Not you as well. This is no time for jokes. As I was saying, Malcolm the Cat, I need to send you under the library to find out why it is tipping over. **Ow!**" he added as a *napoletana* pie hit him in the face.

"You don't get away that easily!" shouted Malcolm the Cat, throwing himself at the pizza and grabbing it with his claws. It slid slowly down King Toothbrush Weasel's front, leaving a trail of tomato sauce the whole way.

King Toothbrush Weasel sighed wearily. "On second thought," he said, "I think I'll send someone more sensible." And he pulled two pairs of dark glasses out of his pocket and ceremoniously placed one on Stinkbomb's face, and the other on Ketchup-Face's.

"Stinkbomb and Ketchup-Face," he said regally, "I hereby appoint you honorary **secret agents** in the Great Kerfuffle **Secret Service.**"

"**Wowsers my trousers!**"

said Stinkbomb eagerly.

"**GOSH my PaNtS!**"

agreed Ketchup-Face, hopping **UP** and **down** with excitement.

"Your mission," King Toothbrush Weasel continued, "is to

go under the library, find out what's making it tip over, and put a stop to it. Off you go!"

"But how do we get there?" Stinkbomb wanted to know.

Miss Butterworth pointed. Beneath the edge of the library that had completely lifted away from the ground, there was a hole—a great chasm that sloped sharply downward into blackness.

"I'll come with you!" the little shopping cart said bravely. Without a moment's hesitation Stinkbomb and Ketchup-Face leapt into the basket, and together the three heroes trundled into the dark.

CHAPTER 14

—•—

IN WHICH
MISS BUTTERWORTH
TAKES A PHONE CALL

King Toothbrush Weasel and Miss Butterworth were still waving good-bye, and Malcolm the Cat was still chasing a slice of *napoletana* around the village square, when they became aware of a ringing sound.

"Is that a telephone?" asked King Toothbrush Weasel.

"Where is it?" Miss Butterworth asked.

"Here it is," said the elephant, taking a phone from a nearby paragraph and passing it over. "I'd answer it myself, but I'm an elephant."

Miss Butterworth answered the phone. *"Hello?"* she said. She paused, listening to the caller at the other end, and said, *"Yes, this is Chapter Fourteen. Miss Butterworth speaking."* She listened some more, interjecting with, *"Goodness! What was that?"* Again she paused, listening. *"It sounded very loud. . . . I see. . . . I shall do my best. Where are you?"* She listened again as the caller told her. *"Oh, dear. Where exactly will that be? I see. I believe I know where that is. . . . I do. Hold on. There's just time. . . ."* Turning to King Toothbrush Weasel, she said, *"I must go,"* and then, mysteriously and silently, she went.

CHAPTER 15

———— • ————

IN WHICH
OUR HEROES PLUNGE
INTO THE DARKNESS

Gosh!" said Stinkbomb. "Is it **Chapter Fifteen** already? **Chapter Fourteen** didn't last long."

"No, it didn't," said Ketchup-Face. Beneath them, the wheels of the little shopping cart trundled onward. Around them, all was dark. "But some chapters are short, aren't they. Do you think this one will be short, too?"

"I expect so," said Stinkbomb.

CHAPTER 16

———— • ————

IN WHICH
OUR HEROES PLUNGE
FARTHER INTO THE DARKNESS

After a bit, Ketchup-Face said, "Do you think our eyes are going to get used to the dark?"

"I don't know," said Stinkbomb.

"Perhaps," suggested the little shopping cart, "if you took your dark glasses off . . . ?"

"Are **secret agents** allowed to take their dark glasses off?" Ketchup-Face asked.

"I should think so," said Stinkbomb. "Like when they're in disguise, or when they go to bed." He took his dark glasses off. "Yes," he said. "That's a bit better."

"Okay," said Ketchup-Face, and she took her dark glasses off too.

And just then, the long dark tunnel down which they were trundling opened up into a large underground cavern, and they saw lights shining in the darkness all around them.

CHAPTER 17

—— • ——

IN WHICH
OUR HEROES DISCOVER
THE LEGENDARY ABANDONED
PIZZA MINES OF GREAT KERFUFFLE

As the little shopping cart trundled to a halt in the middle of the great cavern, the lights began to move toward them. They were miners' lamps, so bright that the wearers' faces could not be seen.

"Hello," Ketchup-Face said bravely. "We're Stinkbomb and Ketchup-Face. We're **secret agents**."

There was a bit of shuffling and muttering among the shadowy figures, and then one of them said, "If you're **secret agents**, how come you're not wearing dark glasses?"

"Um . . . 'cause we're in disguise?" suggested Ketchup-Face.

"But if you were **secret agents** in disguise, you wouldn't tell us you were **secret agents** in disguise, would you? 'Cause then you wouldn't be **secret** anymore. So we don't believe you."

"But if you don't believe us," pointed out Ketchup-Face, "we're still **secret**. So we win!"

"Oh, yeah," said the shadowy figure.

"But if you're **secret agents**," said another

shadowy figure, "what are you doing on that horse?"

"It's not a horse," said Stinkbomb.

"Then why's it got a carrot stuck in its basket?"

"It's another disguise," Stinkbomb explained.

"It's really a horsey called Starlight," added Ketchup-Face helpfully. "But it's disguised as a **secret agent car** disguised as a horsey called Starlight. Who are you?"

"Er, we're moles," said the first shadowy figure.

"Are you really?" said Ketchup-Face, surprised.

"Oh, yes," said the mole. "We're definitely moles. We're very moley indeed. Isn't that right, Rolf the Mole?"

"That's right," agreed Rolf the Mole, a big mole with a big badge that said  . "We're moles all right. Aren't we, Harry the Mole?"

"Yes," agreed Harry the Mole, taking a sip of tea from a mug marked . "We're extremely moley. Aren't we, Stewart the Mole?"

Just as Stewart the Mole was opening his mouth to answer, Harry the Mole passed him a note that said:

Stewart the Mole read it slowly three times and then said, "Er, we're moles." He turned the note over. On the other side it said:

Don't let them know we're moles.

"Er, we're not badgers," he added.

"Oh, good," said Ketchup-Face, reassured.

But Stinkbomb was suspicious. "If you're moles," he asked, "why are you wearing mining helmets? And carrying shovels and pickaxes? I didn't think moles needed shovels and pickaxes."

"Oh, we don't usually," said Stewart the Mole. "Not when we're just digging around looking for . . . um . . . what do moles eat, again?"

"Worms, I think," said Stinkbomb.

"Oh, goody," said Stewart the Mole. "I like

worms. Anyway, we don't need shovels and pick-axes when we're digging for worms. Just when we're mining."

"Mining? What are you mining?" asked Stinkbomb curiously.

"Pizza!"

said the moles excitedly,

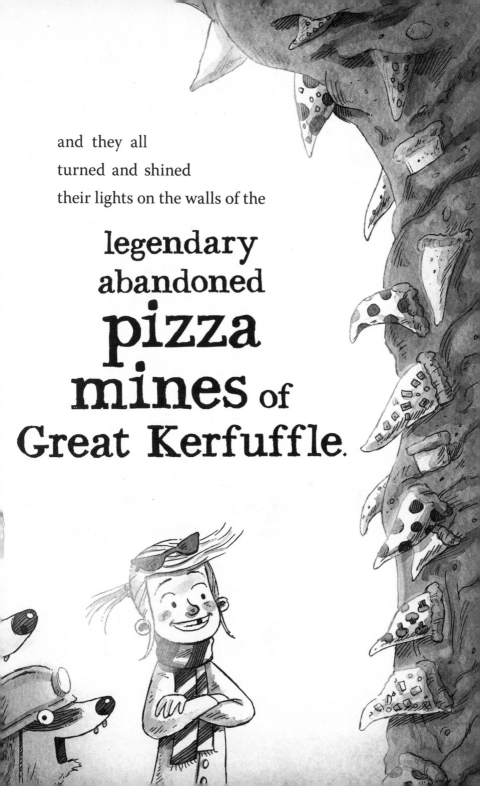

and they all
turned and shined
their lights on the walls of the

legendary
abandoned
pizza
mines of
Great Kerfuffle.

CHAPTER 18

— • —

IN WHICH
STINKBOMB AND KETCHUP-FACE
REMEMBER THEIR MISSION

Stinkbomb and Ketchup-Face gazed around the cavern in awe. In the light of the moles' lamps, the bubbles and crinkles of the pizza crust looked somehow beautiful and mysterious. Here and there, tomato sauce sparkled like rubies; melted cheese shone like gold; olives gleamed like a very precious black thing that's so rare I've never even heard of it. But more than anything, it was the size of the cavern that astounded them.

"A few days ago," said Harry the Mole proudly, "this was just a little tunnel."

"So you've mined *all this* in just a few days?" gasped Stinkbomb. "That's amazing!"

"It's huge!" agreed Ketchup-Face. "It's almost as big as the library!"

"Yes," said Stinkbomb, and then, remembering their mission, added, "The library! We can't stand around here looking at caverns! We've got to save the library!"

"Save the library?" asked Rolf the Mole in a puzzled tone. "What do you mean, save the library?"

"Well," said Stinkbomb importantly, "the Loose Pebbles Library is tipping over, and we have been sent on a **secret mission** to find out why."

"You haven't noticed anything that might be making the library tip over, have you?" added Ketchup-Face.

"Nope," said all the moles, and Stewart the Mole said, "We've been too busy mining this cavern."

"I see," said Ketchup-Face. "So . . . you haven't seen anything that might be making the library tip over, because you've been too busy digging this great big hole under the library?"

"That's right," agreed all the moles.

"Well, that seems fair enough," said Stinkbomb. "We'll just have to keep on looking."

"Um, excuse me," said the little shopping cart shyly.

"Yes?" asked Stinkbomb.

"Well . . ." said the little shopping cart, "it just occurs to me . . . I mean, I was thinking . . . well . . . wouldn't something tip over if you dug a great big hole underneath it?"

"Ummm . . . Yes, I suppose it might," said Stinkbomb. "Why do you ask?"

"Well," said the shopping cart hesitantly, "it's just that, um, if something can tip over because you dig a great big hole under it . . ."

"Yes?" said Stinkbomb and Ketchup-Face and all the moles.

". . . and if the moles have dug a great big hole under the library . . ."

"Yes?" said Stinkbomb and Ketchup-Face and all the moles.

". . . then do you think the library might be tipping over because the moles have dug a great big hole under it?"

Stinkbomb and Ketchup-Face and all the moles thought about this. "Oh, *yeah*!" they said after a moment.

"Then that means," added Ketchup-Face after another moment, "that you ought to stop mining pizzas!"

"Awwww!"

said all the moles, and Stewart the Mole said, "Does it? Why?"

"Well," explained Stinkbomb, "if you keep making the cavern bigger, then the library will tip over, and then the whole island will overturn, and everybody will drown in the sea."

"That would be a shame," said Harry the Mole. "We'd better stop mining, then."

"Fair enough," said all the moles.

"Oh," said Ketchup-Face. "That was easier than I thought."

"Yes," said Stinkbomb. "I sort of thought there might be more of an exciting part at this point."

"Like what?" asked Rolf the Mole.

"I don't know, really," said Stinkbomb. "Like, maybe, I don't know . . . like maybe it turns out that you're really the badgers, and you won't stop mining, so we have to defeat you. Something like that."

"Oh," said Stewart the Mole. "Well, we're not the badgers."

"Er, we are, actually," admitted Rolf the Mole, who was really Rolf the Badger.

"Oh, are we?" said Stewart the Mole, who was really Stewart the Badger. "Oh, yeah. I forgot."

"Gosh," said Stinkbomb. "That was unexpected. I mean, I was just giving an example. I didn't think you really were the badgers. Does that mean we have to defeat you?"

"Nope," said Harry the Mole, who was really

Harry the Badger. "We really are going to stop mining. Aren't we?"

All the badgers nodded.

"But . . . aren't you making lots of money from mining pizzas?" Ketchup-Face asked.

"We were," agreed Harry the Badger sadly.

"And isn't that more important to you than anything else?"

Harry the Badger thought about this. "Nope," he said. "Not if it means the island tipping over and everybody drowning in the sea. We may be **evil** and **wicked**, but we're not *that* **evil** and **wicked**."

"So . . . is that the end of the story, then?" asked Ketchup-Face.

"I suppose so," said Stinkbomb. "It's not a very *good* ending, is it?"

CHAPTER 19

— • —

IN WHICH
IT ISN'T THE END OF
THE STORY AFTER ALL

W ait a minute," said Stinkbomb. "This looks like a new chapter. Maybe it isn't the end of the story."

"But we've saved Great Kerfuffle!" said Ketchup-Face. "The library isn't going to tip over, because there isn't going to be any more mining!"

"Oh, **yes** there **is!**"

growled a menacing voice.

And suddenly Stinkbomb and Ketchup-Face felt themselves seized by the arms. From around them came the clang of shovels and pickaxes and mining helmets being dropped on the ground.

yelped Ketchup-Face. "Let go, you naughty badgers!"

"We haven't got you!" protested Rolf the Badger. "Somebody's got us!"

"Indeed we have," said the voice, and suddenly the cavern was flooded with light. Whoever the mysterious speaker was, he had apparently brought a set of very powerful floodlights with him. Or perhaps his friends had, because Stinkbomb and Ketchup-Face, dazzled as they were by the brightness, could still tell that the cavern was a lot more full than they had expected. Blinking, they realized that the newcomers were . . .

. . . more badgers.

"Oh," said Stinkbomb. "This could get very confusing."

"Allow me to introduce myself," the strange badger went on coldly. "My name is Enrico il Tasso, and I am the leader of the international gang of badgery naughtiness known as the **International Gang of Badgery Naughtiness**. We have come to steal all your underground pizza."

"But you can't, you naughty badgers!" said Ketchup-Face. "If you do any more mining, the library will tip right over and the island will over-turn and we'll all be drownded!"

"Not all of us," said Enrico il Tasso, opening a big box and taking out a submarine. "Is that not so, Rodolfo il Tasso?"

"It is indeed, Enrico il Tasso," said Rodolfo il Tasso, a big badger with a big badge that said

"But first, we must get rid of these badgers and their friends."

"I wouldn't say we're their *friends*," said Stinkbomb.

"Seeing as they're very naughty, and do **evil** and **wicked** doings," added Ketchup-Face.

"Yeah," agreed Harry the Badger. "We're the bad guys."

Enrico il Tasso laughed scornfully. "Ha! *We* are the bad guys now. Are we not, Stefano il Tasso?"

"Are we?" asked Stefano il Tasso, the smallest member of the **International Gang of Badgery Naughtiness**.

Enrico il Tasso passed him a note that said:

Noi
siamo
i cattivi
ora.

Which means, *We are the bad guys now.*

Stefano il Tasso read the note. "Oh, yes," he said. "We are most certainly the bad guys now. **Ah ha** ha ha ha ha ha ha ha ha."

Enrico il Tasso regarded him coldly. "What do you mean, **Ah ha ha ha ha** ha ha ha ha ha?" he asked.

"It's my special bad-guy laugh," Stefano il Tasso explained. "I've been practicing."

"Well, don't," said Enrico il Tasso. "It sounds **stupid**. How is anybody going to take us seriously if you make **stupid** noises like that?"

Stefano il Tasso looked at the ground. "Sorry," he muttered.

"Anyway," said Enrico il Tasso . . .

. . . but just then, his phone rang.

CHAPTER 20

—•—

IN WHICH
ENRICO IL TASSO TAKES A PHONE CALL

Excuse me," said Enrico il Tasso, taking a lovely, shiny, fancy-looking phone out of his pocket. "Hello?" he said. "Ah, excellent. Thank you," and he hung up. "My apologies," he said. "That was my associate on board the ship."

"What ship?" asked Stinkbomb curiously.

Enrico il Tasso smiled unpleasantly. "It is a very big ship called SS *A Very Big Ship*, and it is bringing me the very best and most expensive mining equipment. This equipment is so fast that it can dig out all the pizzas in the pizza mines, cut them up, put them in boxes, and load them into the submarine before the island has finished overturning. It may even have time to sweep up all the pizza crumbs and put them in the trash can, although that will of course be a waste of time, as we will simply knock the trash can over again."

"Gosh," said Stinkbomb, impressed.

"Well," continued Enrico il Tasso, looking at Stinkbomb and Ketchup-Face and the little shopping cart and all the Great Kerfuffle badgers, "it has been lovely meeting you. Now I must send you to your doom."

"Oooh!" said Stewart the Badger excitedly. "What's a doom? Is it a bit like a restaurant?"

"But what about these children, Enrico il Tasso?" asked Rodolfo il Tasso. "Will their parents not be nearby?"

"Oh, no," said Ketchup-Face. "They like to keep out of the way when we're in a story. 'Cause parents spoil stories if they're in them, not letting you go off and be a **secret agent** and explore dangerous holes in the ground and things."

"Are we in a story?" said Enrico il Tasso worriedly. "Oh, dear. Do I look menacing enough?"

"Oh, yes," Stinkbomb assured him. "You look really quite sinister."

Enrico il Tasso sighed with relief. "Good," he said. "Now, where were we?"

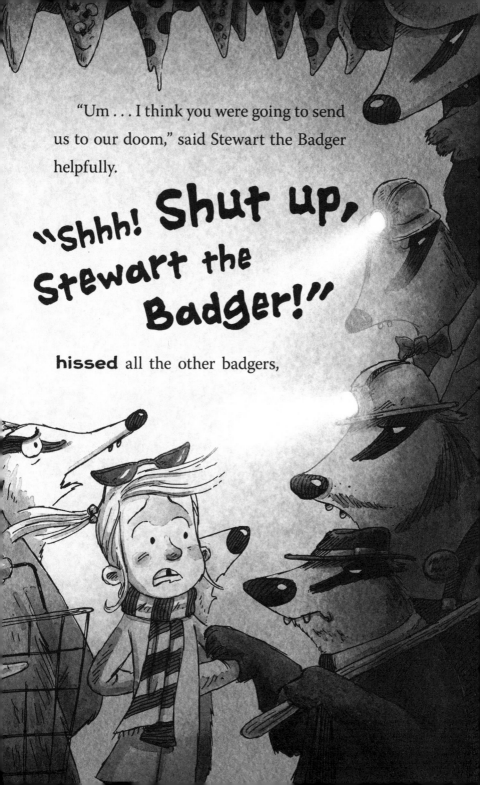

"Um . . . I think you were going to send us to our doom," said Stewart the Badger helpfully.

"Shhh! Shut up, Stewart the Badger!"

hissed all the other badgers,

who did not want to be sent to their doom. But it was too late; Enrico il Tasso had heard.

"Oh, yes," he said. "We shall stack you all into your friend the little shopping cart and push you **down** a very long and dangerous tunnel. This tunnel goes **down** and **down** and **down** very steeply, and then it goes **up** quite a long way, and then just when you think it has finished, it suddenly goes **down** and **down** and **down** and **down** and **down** and **down** and right around in a scary sort of loop-the-loop and **down** and **down** and **down** and **down** and **down** and **down** and **down** and **down** and **down** and **down** and *then . . ."*

Enrico il Tasso paused, and looked around triumphantly.

"*Then*," he continued, "it goes **up** and **up** and **up** and **up** and **up** and **up** and **up** and **up** and **up** and **up** and **up** and **up** and **up** and **up** and **up**, until you come shooting out the other end."

"And where *is* the other end?" asked Stinkbomb.

"Chapter Twenty-Three," said Enrico il Tasso.

"Oh," said Stinkbomb. "That doesn't sound so bad."

"Oh, it is!" said Enrico il Tasso. "Because **Chapter Twenty-Three** begins with a hole high up in the cliffs on the coastline of Great Kerfuffle and finishes with a terrifying plunge toward certain doom in a hostile ocean."

Stinkbomb thought about this. The idea of being stacked into his friend the little shopping cart and pushed **down** a very long and dangerous tunnel that goes **down** and **down** and **down** very steeply, and then goes **up** quite a long way, and then just when you think it has finished suddenly goes **down** and **down** and **down** and **down** and **down** and **down** and right around in a scary sort of loop-the-loop and **down** and **down** and **down** and **down** and **down** and **down** and **down** and **down** and **down** and **down** and **down** and **up** and **up** and **up** and **up** and **up** and **up** and **up** and **up** and **up** and **up** and **up** and **up** and **up** and **up**, until you come shooting out the other end in **Chapter Twenty-Three**, which begins with a hole high up in the cliffs on the coastline of Great Kerfuffle and finishes with a terrifying plunge toward certain doom in a hostile ocean, certainly sounded interesting, but he wasn't sure he would actually like it. So he decided to try to escape.

But the moment he tugged his arm free of the badger who was holding it, all the members of the **International Gang of Badgery Naughtiness** who weren't holding Ketchup-Face, or the little shopping cart, or one of the Great Kerfuffle badgers, jumped on him.

"**Oof!**" he said, and then he and Ketchup-Face were stacked on top of all the Great Kerfuffle badgers in the little shopping cart, and they were wheeled to the very long and dangerous tunnel and pushed **down** it.

CHAPTER 21

— • —

IN WHICH
STINKBOMB AND KETCHUP-FACE TAKE A DEADLY CART RIDE DOWN A DANGEROUS TUNNEL

Aaaaaaaaa Aaaaaaaaaa aaa!!!!!!!!!!!!!!!!!"

yelled Stinkbomb and Ketchup-Face and the little shopping cart and all the badgers—except for

Stewart the Badger, who hadn't quite gotten the hang of what was going on, and who went

"Wheeeeeee!"

instead.

"Can't you just stop?" Stinkbomb yelled from his position on top of the pile of badgers.

"No!" the little shopping cart yelled back. "The tunnel's too steep, and they gave me a very big push! I'm going too fast!"

"And we're getting faster!" moaned Rolf the Badger.

There was nothing they could do. The little shopping cart hurtled **down** and **down** and **down**, picking up speed as it went, so that by the time the tunnel turned and began to climb, they were still racing far, far too fast to stop. **Up** they climbed, quite a long way, with the badgers screaming in terror, and Stinkbomb and Ketchup-Face trying desperately to come up with a clever plan.

"Wait!" cried the little shopping cart. "I think . . . I think I'm slowing down!"

All the badgers stopped screaming. "Oh, yeah!" they said. "Yay!"

"That's lucky!" said Stinkbomb.

"Phew!" said Ketchup-Face.

The little shopping cart rolled upward, gradually losing speed.

"That was scary," said the little shopping cart. "But we're really slowing down now. I should be able to stop in a moment."

cried everyone.

And then the ground dropped away sharply beneath them, and everyone screamed as they suddenly plummeted **down**

and **down**

and **down**

and **down**

and **down**

and **down** · · ·

CHAPTER 22

—·—

IN WHICH
STINKBOMB AND KETCHUP-FACE AND THE LITTLE SHOPPING CART AND THE BADGERS ARE ONLY ONE CHAPTER AWAY FROM A TERRIFYING PLUNGE TOWARD CERTAIN DOOM IN A HOSTILE OCEAN

Aaaaaaaaaa Aaaaaaaaaa aaa!!!!!!!!!!!!!!"

yelled Stinkbomb and Ketchup-Face and the little
shopping cart and all the badgers again as they

raced helplessly **down** the increasingly steep and terrifyingly dangerous tunnel.

"If only I had brakes!" wailed the little shopping cart.

Stinkbomb quickly searched in his pockets for brakes, but he didn't have any.

"Or a big hook on a rope!" Ketchup-Face added.

Stinkbomb searched his pockets for a grappling hook, but he didn't have one of those, either. "And we don't even have a phone!" he added.

"I've got a phone," said Harry the Badger.

"I didn't know you had a phone, Harry the Badger," said Rolf the Badger.

"Yeah, well, I stole it from Enrico il Tasso," said Harry the Badger, passing it up. "'Cause we hadn't done any **evil** and **wicked** doings for a while, and I wanted to get some practice in. Besides, it's shiny."

"Oooh! shiny!"

said all the badgers.

Grabbing the phone, Stinkbomb quickly dialed a one and a four, and waited for an answer.

"Hello?" he said. **"Is that Chapter Fourteen . . . ?** Oh, Miss Butterworth, thank goodness! It's Stinkbomb here! We're in terrible danger!

AAAAAAAAAAA!!!!!

Sorry, that was us going right around in a scary sort of loop-the-loop. . . . Yes, that was because Ketchup-Face and the little shopping cart and the badgers were all **screaming** too. . . . Anyway, can you help us? . . . We're in **Chapter Twenty-Two**, hurtling down a very long and dangerous tunnel toward certain doom in **Chapter Twenty-Three**. . . . Where exactly will the doom be? I'm not sure *exactly*, but it begins with a hole high up in the cliffs on the coastline of Great Kerfuffle and finishes with a terrifying plunge toward certain doom in a hostile ocean. . . . You do? . . . Hurry, Miss Butterworth! You're our only hope!"

He ended the call and said to the others, "Try not to panic! Help is on the way!"

"But will it get here in time?" the little shopping cart called back anxiously.

And then Ketchup-Face screamed,

"Stinkbomb! Look!"

Stinkbomb looked. After the sort of loop-the-loop, they had gone **up** and **up** and **up** and **up** and **up** and **up** and **up** and **up** and **up** and **up** and **up** and **up**, leaving them with only three more **ups** to go before the end of the chapter. Ahead of them, they could see light at the end of the tunnel, and although light at the end of a tunnel is usually a good thing, in this case it wasn't. On the other side of the end of the tunnel was **Chapter Twenty-Three**, and a terrifying plunge toward certain doom in a hostile ocean.

They went **up** and **up** and **up** . . .

CHAPTER 23

— · —

IN WHICH
STINKBOMB AND KETCHUP-FACE
AND THE LITTLE SHOPPING CART AND THE BADGERS
FACE A TERRIFYING PLUNGE TOWARD
CERTAIN DOOM IN A HOSTILE OCEAN

Aaaaaaaaaaa
Aaaaaaaaaaaa
aaa!!!!!!!!!!!!!!!!!!''

yelled Stinkbomb and Ketchup-Face and the little shopping cart and all the badgers, for the third time in as many chapters, as they shot out of a hole high up in the cliffs on the coastline of Great Kerfuffle.

High into the cold sky they soared. The cruel wind whistled in their ears, and sang through their hair, and said a rude poem up their noses. Higher and higher they rose, in a graceful arc over the hostile sea, and then . . .

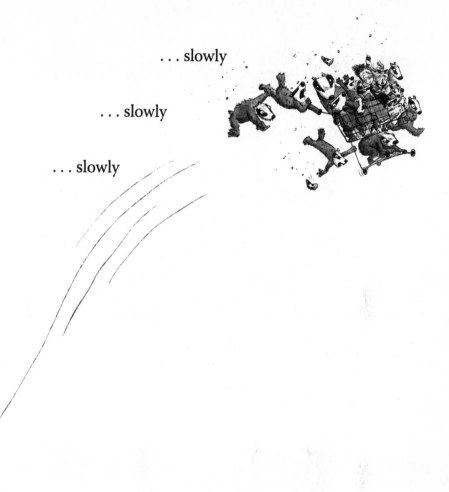

. . . slowly

. . . slowly

. . . slowly

. . . they felt their path through the air reach the top of its curve and begin to curl downward, and suddenly they were falling, falling, falling toward the savage stormy waves below.

"Aaaaaaaaaaaaaaaaaaaaa!!!!!!!!!!!"

they yelled once more as they fell, tumbling and twisting and turning helplessly, spiraling, spinning, somersaulting at sickening speed, dropping down toward the deadly depths of the merciless ocean, until, **howling with despair and terror**, they hit the surface of the sea with the most enormous and unbelievable

CHAPTER 24

—•—

IN WHICH,
QUITE UNEXPECTEDLY,
NOBODY IS DEAD

"Hang on!" Stinkomb said.
"**Boingggggggg**? Shouldn't that have
been **Splashhhhhhhh**?" he asked, rising up
into the air.

"Yes," agreed Ketchup-Face, from somewhere slightly above him, "and what are we doing being all dry up here, instead of being all wet down there?"

"Wheeeeeeeee!"

went all the badgers, reaching the top
of their bounce and dropping back down for
another go.

"Saved!" said the little shopping cart happily, doing a little somersault in midair without actually meaning to.

"I like being sent to my doom," said Stewart the Badger. "It's bouncy!"

Boingggggg!!! went the thing that went *boing* as they all landed on it and bounced back up again, only not quite so high this time, and then it went *Boinggggg!!* as they landed on it again, and then it went *Boinggggg!!* as they landed on it again, and then it went *Boinggggg!* as they landed on it again, and then it went **Boingggg!** as they landed on it again, and then it went **Boinggg! Boingg! Boing!**

And then they all lay there catching their breath and wondering what such an enormous bouncy castle was doing in the middle of the ocean. Except for the badgers, who were wondering what would happen if you put a very big garbage can on a bouncy castle and knocked it over.

CHAPTER 25

— · —

IN WHICH
THE INCREDIBLE RESCUE IS EXPLAINED,
AND THE STORY BEGINS TO MOVE TOWARD
ITS EXCITING CLIMAX

They had not been lying there for very long when a voice like the tinkling of wind chimes called to them.

"*Are you all right?*" it said.

"Miss Butterworth!" Stinkbomb and Ketchup-Face cried happily, leaping to their feet and immediately falling over again. Struggling over to the side of the bouncy castle, they pulled themselves upright and peered over the side.

There, just on the other side of the bouncy

126

wall, they saw Miss Butterworth, sitting on the back of a shark.

"Felicity!" Stinkbomb and Ketchup-Face exclaimed, recognizing their brave and noble hammerheaded friend.

"Hello, you two!" Felicity said, her voice slightly muffled through a mouthful of rope. The other end of the rope was tied to the bouncy castle.

"You saved us!" said the little shopping cart, who had carefully wheeled over to join them.

"Wheeeeeee!" added the badgers, who had all quite recovered and were having a nice bounce on the bouncy castle.

"Calling me in Chapter Fourteen was wise," Miss Butterworth said. *"It gave me just enough time to get this magnificent bouncy castle out here. You are safe now, and you have caught the badgers. All is well."*

"No, it isn't!" Stinkbomb said.

"There are some even **badder** badgers than the **bad** badgers, who aren't being as **bad** as usual, because even though they're **bad**, they're not *that* **bad**, but the really **bad** badgers *are* that **bad**, and we haven't caught them yet!" added Ketchup-Face.

"I see," said Miss Butterworth, and then added, *"No, I don't. Could you explain in another way?"*

"Yes," said Ketchup-Face confidently. "I could explain in a song. I'm good at making up songs." And she began to sing. This is what she sang:

"OH, the INternationaL GanG
of BaDGery NaughtiNess

Are causing everybody
an awful Lot of STRESS

'Cause they want to steal the PizZas
from under Great KerFUFFLE

AND they pushed us
DOWN a tuNNEL after a bit of a

SCUFFLE

If we DoN't stop them they'LL tip the
islaND into the SEEEEEEEEA

AND I'M Not going to sing anymore 'cause
we have to HURR-yyyyyyyyy

No, I'M Not going to sing anymore
'cause we have to HURR-yyyyyyyyy

No, I'M Not going to sing anymore
'cause we have to

HURR-yyyyyyyyyyy..."

CHAPTER 26

—— • ——

IN WHICH
WE SKIP TO THE END OF KETCHUP-FACE'S
SONG IN ORDER TO SAVE PAPER

No, I'm not going to sing anymore 'cause we have to HURR-yyyyyyyy,"

Ketchup-Face continued.

"No, I'm not going to sing anymore 'cause we have to HURR-yyyyyyyyy

No, I'm not going to sing anymore 'cause we have to HURR-yyyyyyyyy

No, I'm not going to sing anymore 'cause we have to HURR-yyyyyyyyy . . ."

Several minutes later, after she had repeated the line about having to hurry another sixty-seven times, Ketchup-Face sang it all twice more. Then she did a bit that went "Dooby-dooby-dooby-dooby" for rather a long time, and then she did the first bit again, and then she sang the whole lot three more times before finally getting to the big finish:

♪ "No, I'm . . . NOT!!!!!!! GOING TO SING!!!!!!!! ANYMORE!!!!!!!!!!!!! BECAUSE WE HAVEN'T GOT TI-I-I-I-I- ♩ /-I-I-I-I-I-I-I- ♩ /-IME!!!!!!!!!!!!!!!!!!!

"That's a song about the **International Gang of Badgery Naughtiness**," she added.

"*Well done*," said Miss Butterworth politely, and then added, "*The International Gang of Badgery Naughtiness! Those villains!*"

"Yes," agreed Stinkbomb. "And—look!"

They looked where he was pointing—except for the badgers, who were all still bouncing up and down and shouting

"wheeeee!"

Coming up rapidly behind them was a very big ship. They could see the name painted proudly on its prow: SS *A Very Big Ship*.

"That's the ship bringing their mining equipment!" exclaimed Ketchup-Face.

"Quickly!" said Stinkbomb. "We need a plan!" And he and Ketchup-Face and the little shopping cart and Miss Butterworth and Felicity all put their heads together, except for the little shopping cart, who didn't actually have a head but who still joined in the planning. There was a lot of muttering that nobody else could hear over the noise of the waves splashing against the side of the bouncy castle, and the engines of SS *A Very Big Ship* drawing closer, and the badgers going

"wheeeee!"

and the bouncy castle going

Boinggggg!

Then Miss Butterworth said, *"Very well. Are you ready?"*

Stinkbomb and Ketchup-Face and the little shopping cart all gulped a little nervously, and said, "Yes."

Stinkbomb and Ketchup-Face scrambled back into the basket of the little shopping cart. Miss Butterworth climbed over the side of the bouncy

castle and, lifting them, she began to bounce higher and higher, each bounce taking them farther into the sky.

And then, just as it seemed they could go no higher, Miss Butterworth hurled them with all her ninja librarian strength, and they felt themselves soar into the air.

Above them, they saw the hole high up in the cliffs on the coastline of Great Kerfuffle. They saw its black mouth growing closer and closer.

And then it swallowed them up.

CHAPTER 27

— • —

IN WHICH
THEY TRAVEL BACK THROUGH THE TUNNEL

This time, nobody screamed. Stinkbomb and Ketchup-Face put on their dark glasses and sat, upright and serious, in the little shopping cart. There was no noise except for the trundling of the little shopping cart's wheels, and Ketchup-Face humming some exciting **secret agent music**, and Stinkbomb pretending to talk into a **secret agent radio**.

They went **down** and **down** and **down** and **down** and **down** and **down** and **down** and **down** and **down** and **down** and **down** and

down and **down** and **down** and **up** and **up** and **up** and **up** and **up** and **up** and **up** and **up** and **up** and **up** and right around in a scary sort of loop-the-loop and **up** and **up** and **up** and **up** and **up** and **up** and

        d

           o

              w

                  n

quite a long way and then **up** and **up** and **up**, and then they came bursting out of the tunnel and landed right on top of Enrico il Tasso.

CHAPTER 28

— • —

IN WHICH
STINKBOMB AND KETCHUP-FACE
LAND ON ENRICO IL TASSO,
AND THERE ISN'T AN ELEPHANT

"Oof!"
said Enrico il Tasso.

CHAPTER 29

— · —

IN WHICH
ENRICO IL TASSO GETS UP

Enrico il Tasso looked up at Stinkbomb and Ketchup-Face. "Could you get off me, please?" he said coldly.

"Sorry," said the little shopping cart, and trundled carefully backward.

Enrico il Tasso stood, and brushed himself down. "So," he said. "You escaped your doom."

"Well, it *is* a **secret agent story**," Stinkbomb pointed out. "**Secret agents** usually do escape their doom in **secret agent stories**."

"Do they?" said Enrico il Tasso. "I don't read

many **secret agent stories**. I prefer stories with people getting married and kissing each other."

The other badgers sniggered.

Enrico il Tasso blushed. "Er, no," he said. "I mean . . . I prefer crime stories with lots of fighting, where the bad guy gets away at the end. Anyway, now that you are back, what are we going to do with you?"

"The question is," said Stinkbomb coolly, "what are *we* going to do with *you*?"

"Yeah!" said Ketchup-Face excitedly, flashing her library card like a secret agent badge.

"you're all under arrest, suckers!"

"No, we are not," said Enrico il Tasso.

"Oh," said Ketchup-Face. "Why not?"

"Well," said Enrico il Tasso, "because there are many more of us than there are of you."

"Oh," said Ketchup-Face. "Well . . . in that case . . . would you like to hear a song?"

"We have no time to listen to songs," said Enrico il Tasso. "We have to get on with mining all this pizza and making your island overturn."

"But the mining equipment hasn't arrived yet," pointed out Rodolfo il Tasso.

"And we do like music," Stefano il Tasso added.

Enrico il Tasso narrowed his eyes and looked at Ketchup-Face. He had found Harry the Badger's copy of STINKBOMB AND KETCHUP-FACE AND THE BADNESS OF BADGERS in the tunnels, and had been reading it. "It's not the one about blueberry jam, is it?" he asked suspiciously.

"Oh, no," said Ketchup-Face innocently. "It's a new one. It's about the **International Gang of Badgery Naughtiness**."

"**Ooooh!**" said the **International Gang of Badgery Naughtiness** excitedly. They'd never been in a song before.

"And if you really like music," Ketchup-Face added, "I could teach you to sing it."

"Oooh!" said all the members of the **International Gang of Badgery Naughtiness** again. "Could we? *Plee*-ease?"

Enrico il Tasso sighed. "Well," he said, "just while we're waiting for the mining equipment."

CHAPTER 30

— • —

IN WHICH
THE INTERNATIONAL GANG OF BADGERY NAUGHTINESS LEARNS KETCHUP-FACE'S NEW SONG, AND SOMETHING UNEXPECTED HAPPENS

It took a very long time for Ketchup-Face to teach the song, partly because she kept changing the tune as she went along, and partly because some of the **International Gang of Badgery Naughtiness** kept adding in little ideas of their own. Not only that, but Rodolfo il Tasso was very fond of opera, and insisted that Ketchup-Face's ending wasn't long or dramatic enough, and made her add some more.

But eventually the **International Gang of Badgery Naughtiness** had finished learning the song, and they sang it a few times until it sounded really quite good, or at least not completely dreadful. And then Ketchup-Face said, "I know! Let's have a concert!"

"All right," sighed Enrico il Tasso. "But only until the mining equipment gets here. Where can it be? Has anybody seen my phone?"

And just then, Enrico il Tasso's phone beeped—but very softly, like the tinkling of wind chimes. Only Stinkbomb heard it, because it was in his pocket. When nobody was looking, he slipped it out and glanced at the screen. On it was a single word:

He nodded at Ketchup-Face. It was a **secret-agenty** sort of nod, and she understood at once what it meant, because she was being a **secret agent** as well. Quickly, she organized the **International Gang of Badgery Naughtiness** into rows along one of the walls.

"This is the stage," she said, "and you have to stand like this."

When they were all ready, Stinkbomb stepped forward. "Just before you do the concert," he said, "this is your last chance to surrender."

"Surrender?" said Enrico il Tasso scornfully. "You don't seem to understand. We have won! The only thing stopping your island from flipping over is the fact that the library is tied to an elephant. And even the elephant will not be able to hold it once we have finished digging out all the pizza that is holding the library up."

"Sorry I'm late," said the elephant. "I was supposed to be in **Chapter Twenty-Eight**, but there was a library tied to my ankle."

The **International Gang of Badgery Naughtiness** stared.

"Where did you appear from?" asked Rodolfo il Tasso.

"And . . . if you are here," asked Enrico il Tasso, "who is holding up the library?"

The elephant shrugged. "Dunno," it said. "Miss Butterworth just chopped the rope with her big sword and said I could go now."

"But that means . . . !" said Enrico il Tasso.

And just then, they heard a noise. It was an ominous noise, like the sound of a library sliding **down** a long dark tunnel, getting quicker and quicker and closer and closer.

CHAPTER 31

—◦—

IN WHICH
THE CLEVER PLAN REACHES
ITS FULFILLMENT

W hat?" said Enrico il Tasso. "No! It is impossible!"

The ominous sliding noise got louder and louder. It was coming from the tunnel that led to the surface.

"Run!" shouted Enrico il Tasso. "Run, or be **squashed** by a library!"

But there was nowhere to run. And before they had a chance to move, the enormous building rushed from the mouth of the tunnel.

"Aaaa
aaaaa
aaaaaa
aaa!!!!!!!!!.....

aaaaa aaaa aaaaaaa !!!!"

yelled Enrico il Tasso and Rodolfo il Tasso and Stefano il Tasso and all the rest of the **International Gang of Badgery Naughtiness** as the vast structure bore down on them and squashed them against the cavern wall with a deafening...

CHAPTER 32

IN WHICH
THE INTERNATIONAL GANG
OF BADGERY NAUGHTINESS
IS DEFEATED

It was not the library at all. It was the bouncy castle. As it bounced back from the cavern wall, all the members of the **International Gang of Badgery Naughtiness** went **"Bleeeeeugh"** and fell to the floor, stunned. Before they could move, Miss Butterworth, King Toothbrush Weasel, Malcolm the Cat, and all the Great Kerfuffle badgers bounced out of the bouncy castle, jumped on the international badgers, and tied them up.

"Hooray!" shouted Stinkbomb, Ketchup-Face, and the little shopping cart, jumping **up** and **down**. And then, remembering that they were **secret agents**, they stopped jumping **up** and **down** and shouting, "Hooray!" and instead just stood around looking cool and saying things like, "Well done. Good job."

"wheeeee!" said all the Great Kerfuffle badgers, getting back on the bouncy castle and jumping **up** and **down**.

"Now," said King Toothbrush Weasel, "what

shall we do with these naughty international badgers?"

"Ah," said the elephant. "This is where I come in. Allow me to introduce myself," it continued, putting on a pair of dark glasses and a foreign accent. "**Double-O Alessandro l'Elefante** at your service. I am a **secret agent**, and I have been sent here on a mission to capture these **wicked** badgers, bring them home, and put them in prison."

"Oh, good," said King Toothbrush Weasel.

"I'm very grateful for your help," Alessandro l'Elefante went on. "But tell me—what is holding the library up now?"

"Ah," said Miss Butterworth. *"We got a very long rope and tied it to* SS A Very Big Ship."

"But we can't leave it like that forever," said King Toothbrush Weasel, concerned. "How are we going to stop the library from tipping over and flipping the island upside down?"

"Well," said Alessandro l'Elefante, "I suggest

that the first part of the **International Gang of Badgery Naughtiness**'s punishment is to make enough pizza to completely fill the legendary abandoned pizza mines of Great Kerfuffle."

"*And when that is done,*" said Miss Butterworth wisely, "*I suggest the pizza mines be abandoned again. Forever, this time.*"

"Jolly good idea," said King Toothbrush Weasel. "I shall make a law about that."

"And perhaps," Ketchup-Face suggested, with her sweetest smile—the one that showed where she had recently lost a tooth—"those naughty badgers could make a bit of extra pizza, as well?"

"Or a lot of extra pizza?" suggested Stinkbomb. "We didn't get to finish our lunch."

Alessandro l'Elefante smiled elephantly. "Of course."

"So," said the little shopping cart happily, "I suppose that *is* the end of the story now."

"Not quite," said King Toothbrush Weasel. "There is still the matter of *our* badgers. They did escape from jail. And they are still **evil** and **wicked**."

"Yes," said Ketchup-Face, "but not *that* **evil** and **wicked**. After all, they did stop mining when they found out how dangerous it was. And they did help us to catch the **International Gang of Badgery Naughtiness**."

"True," said King Toothbrush Weasel, and he turned to the bouncy castle and said, "Badgers! The king commands your attention!"

All the badgers looked at King Toothbrush Weasel and stopped going

"wheeeee!"

although they did keep bouncing **up** and **down.**

"In recognition of your selfless sacrifice in stopping mining for pizzas, and in recognition of your invaluable help in jumping on the other badgers and tying them up, you are royally pardoned. You will not have to go back to prison at the end of the story."

"Hooray!" shouted all the bad-gers, and to celebrate, they robbed the bank and painted "Badgers Rule" all over the palace.

"Oh," said King Toothbrush Weasel. "Well, that was very naughty. I'm afraid that you *will* have to go back to prison after all."

"Awwwwww!"

said all the badgers.

"But since you did help us," King Toothbrush Weasel went on, "you can take the bouncy castle with you."

"Hooray!"

shouted all the badgers, and they rushed back to prison with the bouncy castle and started trying to see if they could bounce up as high as the sky-light and escape that way.

CHAPTER 33

———— • ————

IN WHICH
ALL ENDS HAPPILY

Later that evening, Stinkbomb and Ketchup-Face and all their friends gathered in King Toothbrush Weasel's backyard.

As well as Stinkbomb and Ketchup-Face, and of course King Toothbrush Weasel himself, there was the little shopping cart, and Miss Butterworth, and Malcolm the Cat, and Alessandro l'Elefante, and a big crate full of the **International Gang of Badgery Naughtiness**. They all sat contentedly, eating pizza and gazing down at

the peaceful little village of Loose Pebbles, and listening to the distant "**wheeeeeeee!**"s coming from the village jail. And Stinkbomb and Ketchup-Face thought that only one more thing was needed to make their happiness complete.

Then there was a creaking from the gate at the bottom of the yard, and two figures moved quietly through the darkness and hid behind a bush.

Stinkbomb and Ketchup-Face froze, thinking of all those spy stories where one of the bad guys comes back just as you think it's all over and tries to kill the heroes; but then, as the moon rose brightly behind the bush, they saw two familiar shapes silhouetted through the branches.

"Mom! Dad!" cried Stinkbomb.

"Hello, my darlings!" came their mother's voice from behind the bush. "Can we come out? Has the story finished yet?"

"Yes," said Ketchup-Face happily.

"Would you like to try my really yummy pizza?"

How to make Pizza the Ketchup-Face Way
by Ketchup-Face

1. First you need a base for your pizza. Anything round will do—a Frisbee, a piece of cardboard, an old record from when your parents were children about a hundred years ago . . .

You could use a garbage can lid! They're round.

Of course, you'll have to knock the garbage can over first.

Most round things will not do. You can buy a premade pizza crust from a store, or you can make one with flour, salt, yeast, and water. It is easy to find a pizza crust recipe at the library—you can borrow a book or use a library computer to look on the internet.

2. Then cover it with ketchup.

Do not use ketchup.
Use pizza sauce from a can
or jar or find a recipe to make your
own. Do not use too much or the
pizza may turn out soggy.

Or you could just put lots
of tomatoes on your pizza
base and then sit on them.

3. Next, get a block of cheese and put it
on the base.

Grate the cheese first.
Or you can use thin slices of
mozzarella. You can use more than
one type of cheese if you like. Again,
do not use too much.

If you don't have any cheese,
you could just wipe it with
old socks. They can be a
little cheesy sometimes.

4. Add some really yummy toppings. Use something you really like to eat, like chocolate or ice cream.

Traditional toppings are best on a pizza—pepperoni, onions, sausage, peppers. Not chocolate or ice cream.

Worms and rubbish!
Worms and rubbish!

5. Finally, put it in the oven.

Ask a grown-up to help cook the pizza. It should take about ten minutes.

Oh, are you supposed to cook it?
— Burp!

ACKNOWLEDGMENTS

——— • ———

Big thanks go to Sam Churchill and his mom for their generous bid in the Authors for the Philippines auction.

A huge *grazie* to my lovely friend Concetta Perot for casting a critical eye over the non-English words and phrases.

Once more, thanks to all the children from whom I've stolen ideas that have made it into the book.

And, as ever, enormous gratitude to Noah and Cara for their love and inspiration, and for their increasingly specific contributions to the kingdom and inhabitants of Great Kerfuffle.

Jo Cotterill

JOHN DOUGHERTY was born in Larne, Northern Ireland, and not many years later they made him go to school—an experience he didn't find entirely enjoyable. Fortunately, the joys of reading helped him through the difficult times. It's therefore not completely surprising that when he grew up he became first a teacher (the nice sort), and then a writer of stories and poetry to make children giggle. He also writes songs, some of which he performs with First Draft, a band made up of three children's authors and a bookseller. He now lives in England with his two wonderful children, the original Stinkbomb and Ketchup-Face.

Learn more about John at
www.visitingauthor.com